FROGGY'S BEST BABYSITTER

FROGGY'S BEST BABYSITTER

by JONATHAN LONDON
illustrated by FRANK REMKIEWICZ

SCHOLASTIC INC.
New York Toronto London Auckland
Sydney Mexico City New Delhi Hong Kong

For Sandy, Amy, Glenn, Natalia, Aaron, & Sean; and in fond memory of Sarah
  —J.L.

For Daniella, Farmor Bente, Nana Bird, Nana Sylvia, and Grandma Wanda
  —F.R.

ISBN 978-0-545-32849-4

12 11 10 9 8 7 6 5 4 3 2   11 12 13 14 15 16/0

Printed in the U.S.A.   08

This edition first printing, January 2011

Set in Kabel

It was Saturday morning
and Froggy was hungry.
He lay in bed
and dreamed about
French toast
sprinkled with
sugar-coated flies.
Yum!

FRROOGGYY!

called his mother.
"Wha-a-a-a-t?"
"It's time to get up, dear!
Your babysitter's coming!"

Froggy hopped out of bed
and flopped to the kitchen—*flop flop flop*.

"But I don't *want* a babysitter!" cried Froggy.
"I want to come with you!"
"But it's our tenth anniversary, dear!
We're spending *one* night in the city!
Your babysitter will take good care of you."
"But what if she's *mean*?" asked Froggy.

Brriiinnng! Brrriiinnng! rang the doorbell.
"Now meet Sandy, your new babysitter."
"Hi, Froggy! What's up?"

"How come I can't come with you, Mom?"

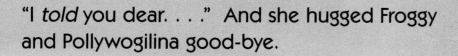

"I *told* you dear. . . ." And she hugged Froggy and Pollywogilina good-bye.

WAAAAAAAAAA!

cried Polly
as soon as they'd left.

Sandy picked her up and sang,
"Rock-a-bye baby . . ."
"I think she's hungry," said Froggy,

and he climbed a stool and—
splish! splash! sizzle! mash!—
he made Polly mashed French toast.
"What a *mess!*" cried Sandy.

But Froggy ate two pieces—all sprinkled
with sugar-coated flies—*munch crunch munch . . .*
then flopped to his room
to get dressed—*flop flop flop.*

"Rats!" said Sandy, when he came back. "My cell phone is dead!"
"Do you have a *boyfriend*?" asked Froggy.
"None of your beeswax!"
Froggy handed her a phone . . .

and snuck into his parents' room and listened in on their phone. "Hi, Danny!" said Sandy.

FRROOGGYY !

called Sandy, after dessert.
"Wha-a-a-t?"
"Art time!"
Froggy plopped down in front of the TV
and said, "Mom always lets us watch
lots and *lots* of TV!"

So for dinner, they had frozen pizza with leftover fly sauce—*munch crunch munch.*

"Mom lets us have *three* desserts!" said Froggy.
"You can't have three," said Sandy.
"But you *can* have a triple banana split with chocolate fly sauce!"
"Num-num!" squealed Polly.

That afternoon, they leapfrogged
all the way to the market—*flop flop flop.*

But when they got home,
Froggy dropped the bag of groceries—*splop!*

Froggy giggled, and sang,
"Sandy and Danny, sitting in a tree

K·I·S·S·I·N·G!

"Get off the phone, *now*!"
screamed Sandy.
"Oops!" said Froggy, laughing
like mad.

"You can't watch TV," said Sandy.
"But you *can* make something with clay!"
"Yippee!" said Froggy.
And while he made a dinosaur, Polly made blobs.
She threw some . . . and ate some . . .
then stuffed one down her diaper.
Froggy rolled over laughing and *smoooooshed*
his dinosaur *a-a-a-a-all* across the carpet.

FRROOGGYY!

yelled Sandy.
"Wha-a-a-a-t?"
"Bath time!"
"But I don't *want* to take a bath!"
"Take a bath or clean the carpet!" she said.

So Froggy took a bath with Polly—
splash splash splash.
He made a suds wig for Polly
and a suds beard for himself.

FRROOGGYY!

called Sandy.
"Wha-a-a-t?"
"Bedtime!"
"But I don't *want* to go to bed!
Mom always lets us stay up
till midnight!"
"Go to bed or mop the floor!"
she said.

So Froggy went to bed.
But Sandy had to read ten books
before he fell asleep—*zzzzzzzzzzzz.*

Then she stayed up past midnight cleaning the house.

And in the morning she woke up to—"*WAAAAAAAAA! FWWWOOGGY!*"
"She's hungry!" said Froggy.
"I'll make French toast!"
"Er, *thanks*, Froggy," said Sandy, "but *I'll* make it! You go play."

It had rained all night,
so Froggy went outside
and jumped in the mud—*slup slup slup.*

When he saw the taxi,
he flopped back inside—
flop flop flop—and yelled,
"They're *commmiiiing!*"

NOOOOOOOOooo...!

howled Sandy.
"You tracked mud all over the carpet!"

"Oops!" cried Froggy,
looking more red in the face
than green.

But then like superfrog,
he swooped up the red carpet
(kept for special guests)

and flung it out—*flooooooooop!*—
and covered his muddy footprints.

And when Mom and Dad came in, he sang,
"*HAPPY ANNIVERSARY!*"
"Wow!" said Mom.
"The house looks great!"
"Yes!" said Dad.
"This is the best anniversary
we've ever had!"

"And Sandy's the best babysitter ever!" said Froggy.
"Wonderful!" said Mom.
"I hope you can babysit again, real soon!"

"Um," said Sandy, waving good-bye.
"Thanks, but I think I'm moving to Australia—
real soon."